Shrimp Joins the Team

by Kathy Furgang
illustrated by Anita DuFalla

"Let's all welcome Jake to our class," said Mrs. Wilson. "He just moved to our town."

Jake stood in front of the class.
It was his first day at this school
and he was feeling a little scared.

Jake heard two girls in the front row.
"He is so short!" said one girl.
"Yeah, a real shrimp," said the other.

Jake sat in the back of the room.
"How's the weather down there?"
asked Mean Marvin. Everyone laughed.

Jake did not like being teased about his height. It made him feel bad. It was not fair. Why was being short so bad?

"Do not forget to sign up
for the baseball team," said Mrs. Wilson.
"It will be fun to play baseball games."

Jake was happy. He liked baseball more than anything.

"Shrimps can't play baseball," said Mean Marvin.

"Don't let them get to you," said Tommy. "They make fun of me, too. I just try to ignore them."

"Why is being short so bad?" asked Jake. The boys couldn't think of a reason.

Jake went to the baseball field after class. "You're not strong enough to lift the bat, Shrimp," they said as they laughed.

"Hey, Shrimp! Let's see if you can throw the ball," said one boy. Jake threw the ball. It sailed far over the boy's head.

They all stopped to look.
Jake could really throw a ball!

Then Jake picked up a bat. He hit a ball right over everyone's head. They couldn't believe their eyes. He could really hit a ball, too!

"Hey, Shrimp, way to go!" they yelled.

Jake helped the team win their first game. “I’m sorry I called you Shrimp,” said Mean Marvin. “It doesn’t matter how tall you are. I’d be lucky to be on your team any day!”